cou

Passing On

by **Mike Dumbleton & Terry Denton**

RED FOX

For Chris, 1952–2000, with love MD
For my parents, TD

Red Fox
an imprint of
Random House Australia Pty Ltd
Level 3, 100 Pacific Highway, North Sydney NSW 2060
http://www.randomhouse.com.au

Sydney New York Toronto
London Auckland Johannesburg
and agencies throughout the world

First published in hardback 2001, reprinted 2002
Red Fox edition 2002, reprinted 2005, 2006, 2008
Text copyright © Mike Dumbleton 2001
Illustrations copyright © Terry Denton 2001

National Library of Australia Cataloguing-in-Publication Data

Dumbleton, Mike.
Passing on.
ISBN 978 0 091 84089 1
ISBN 0 091 84089 9
1. Grandmothers – Juvenile fiction. 2. Children's stories, Australian.
I. Denton, Terry, 1950–. II. Title.

A823.3

Designed by Sandra Nobes
Production: Linda Watchorn
Production coordination: Pia Gerard
Children's Publisher: Linsay Knight
Colour separations: Pica, Singapore
Printer: Sing Cheong Printing Co. Ltd, Hong Kong

My grandma lived with cheerful pride,
down by the docks at Ambleside.

She had a dog, she had a cat,
but Grandma had much more than that.

She had a way of making me
feel grown up, from the age of three.

We painted fences,
planted flowers,
walked and talked
for hours and hours.

We often fished
from off the quay,

to try and catch our lunch for free.
Together we reeled in the line.
She always said the fish was mine.

Sometimes I paddled in the sea,
then Gran would wade in next to me.

Crashing waves, shifting sand,
I liked it when she held my hand.

When I cried she held me tight
and whispered that I'd be all right.
Her voice was calm,
her smile was strong.
I never felt upset for long.

She showed me photos when I asked,
and shared her memories of the past.

The pipe,
the chair,
the crooked cane . . .

made Grandpa come to life again.

She said that I had Grandpa's looks:
his cheeky smile,
his love of books.

It made me feel a little weird and thankful not to have his beard!

Now Gran's passed on,
the house is sold.

The windows look
so bare and cold.

Memories stir inside of me
as Mum drives by towards the sea.

My brother paddles in the foam.
He tries to do it all alone.

Crashing waves,
shifting sand,
make him want to hold my hand.

When he cries I hold him tight
and whisper that he'll be all right.

My voice is calm, my smile is strong.
He never feels upset for long.

And as we stand upon the shore,

I know that Grandma's here once more.

She's with me now
although she's gone,

and the things she did . . .

I'm passing on.